THE BLUE STONE

A JOURNEY THROUGH LIFE

JIMMY LIAO

ENGLISH TEXT ADAPTED BY
SARAH L. THOMSON

LITTLE, BROWN AND COMPANY
OUNG READERS
NEW YORK · BOSTON

Ten thousand years go by,

a thousand years go by,

a hundred years go by,

ten years go by,

a year goes by…

A blue stone lies peacefully

in the heart of a forest.

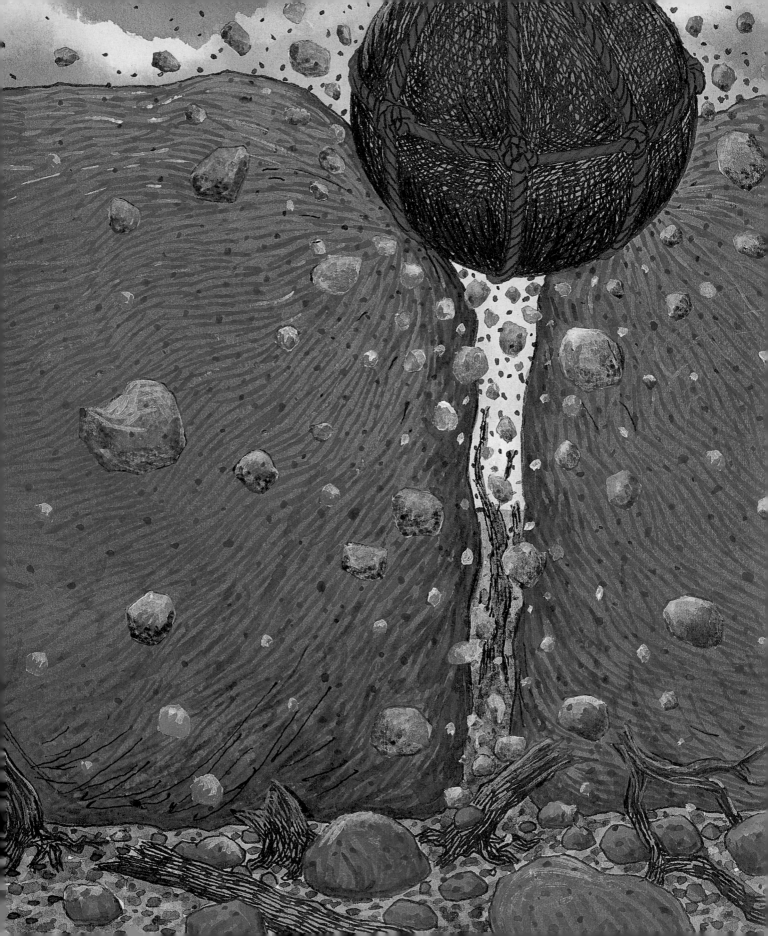

People come to the forest.

They see how beautiful the stone is,

and they love it.

They long for it.

They decide to take it with them,

and they split it in two.

As soon as the stone starts out on its journey,

it longs for its other half.

It wants to go home.

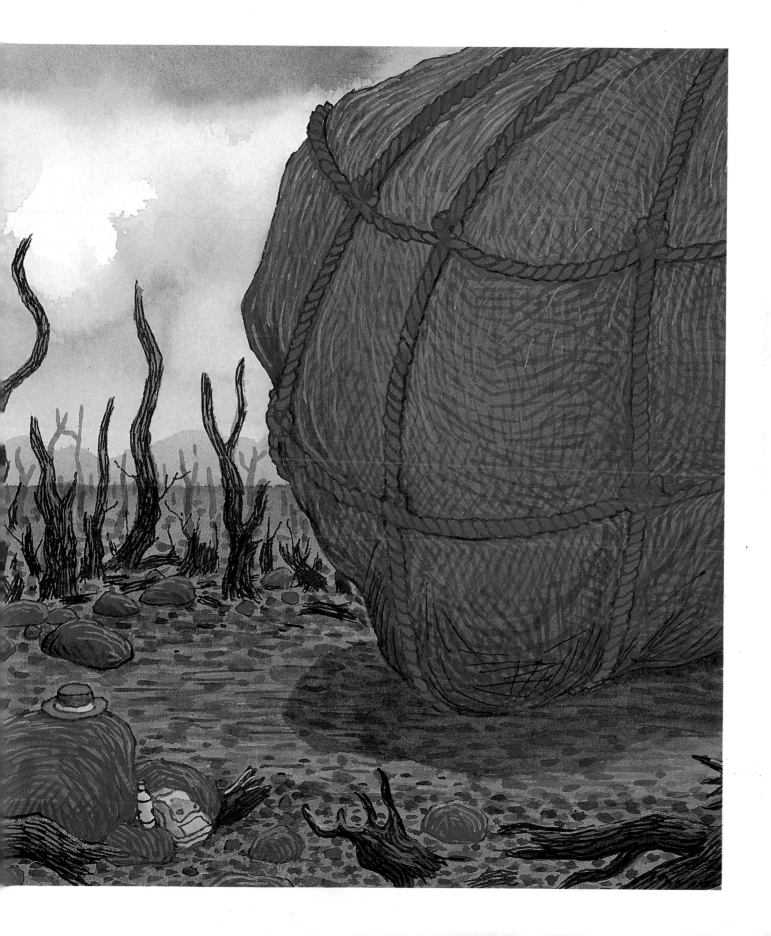

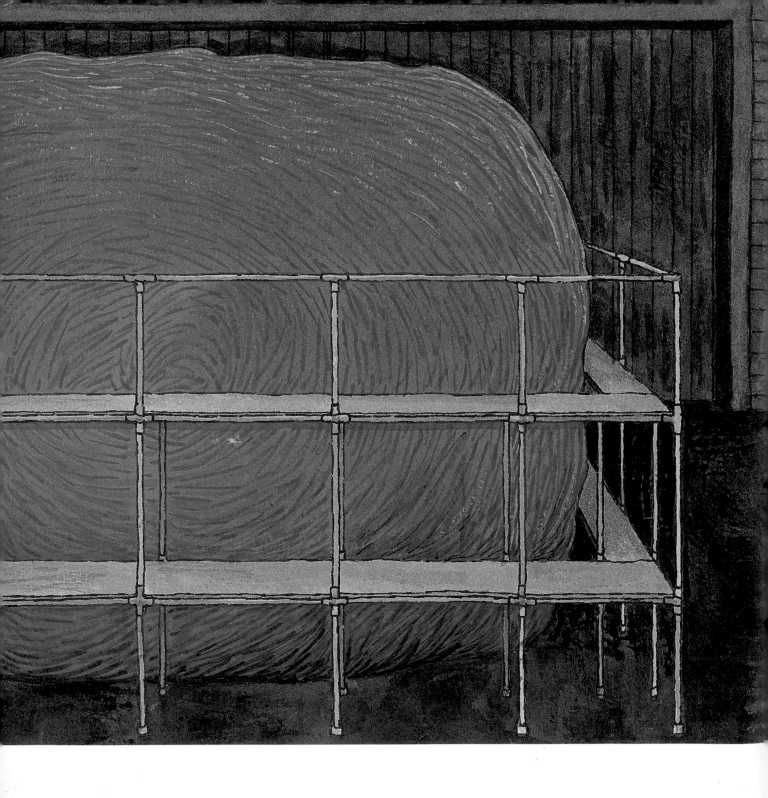

The blue stone waits quietly

in a chilly workshop.

A man with piercing eyes thinks,

and specks of dust float in the sunlight.

A year and a half later

the stone is on its way

to a far-off city.

It arrives in a world

of chatter and noise.

People bubble over with delight

to see what the blue stone has become.

But when night falls,

the stone is alone once more,

until a lost child wanders by.

"Dear stone elephant," he asks,

"can you tell me the way home?"

The stone remembers sunlight on leaves

and small birds fluttering

What's left of the stone

comes to a new artist.

Nine months later,

a statue is ready for a garden.

Every day a lady

hobbles out to smell her flowers

and talk softly to her stone bird.

Years pass, and the lady

never comes to her garden now.

Her grandson finds a broken statue

among weeds and wildflowers.

He carves a new sculpture

for a seaside town.

Every day the stone watches

a young man sail out to sea.

Every day his sweetheart

welcomes him home.

But one day the young man

does not come home.

The girl waits on the dock

while waves smash against the reef

and the cold wind blows.

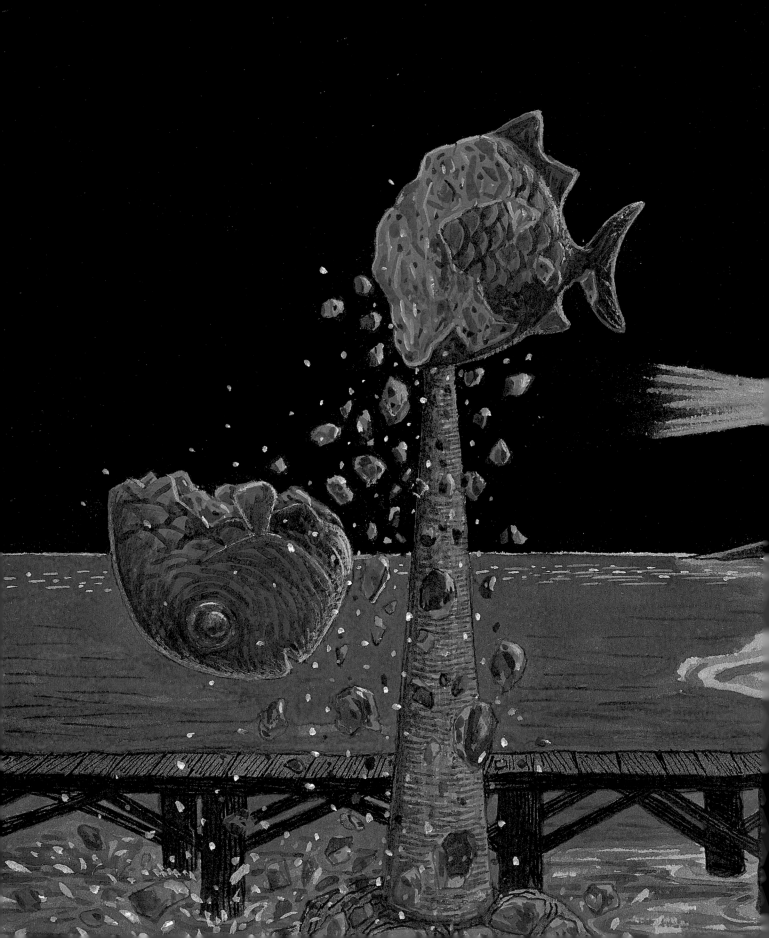

The stone remembers

butterflies resting on it

and wolves sleeping in its shade.

Its heart breaks a little.

It wants to go home.

For long years the stone lies forgotten.

But then two divers swim by.

The stone, they think,

can be made into something new.

They're singing as they carry

the stone to its new home.

But the stone knows

this home is not where it belongs.

The glow of a golden moon

warms people's hearts.

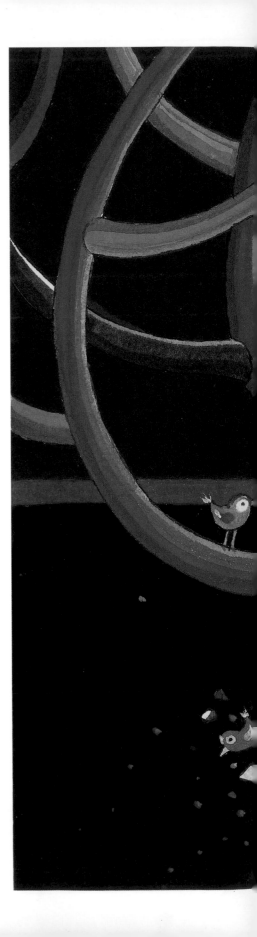

But the stone remembers

the brown backs of bears

disappearing into their dens for winter sleep.

Its heart breaks a little.

It wants to go home.

The broken stone is thrown outside.

It lies in a field

until children discover it.

They take it to a friend

and beg him to carve them something to love.

Soon a sweet-faced stone cat

looks out of an orphanage window.

The cat and the children

gaze at mountains and clouds,

longing for a home they cannot see.

On Christmas Eve, carols float on the wind.

The stone cat sees candlelight

glowing from each house.

The stone remembers snowflakes floating down

to settle on its back.

Its heart breaks a little.

It wants to go home.

Tossed on a trash heap,

the blue stone is found…

...by prisoners who carry rocks

to build their own jail.

The stone can hear their sighs.

Every day a young woman weeps.

Every night she sings.

While she sleeps,

the stone remembers

moonlight painting every blade of grass with silver-gray.

The woman dreams of slipping through the bars,

of flying free on the wind.

She tosses out a stone

to watch it soar.

The blue stone lies at rest

in a forest of falling leaves.

When a circus passes by,

a clown picks up the stone.

With bright paint it makes

a perfect juggling ball.

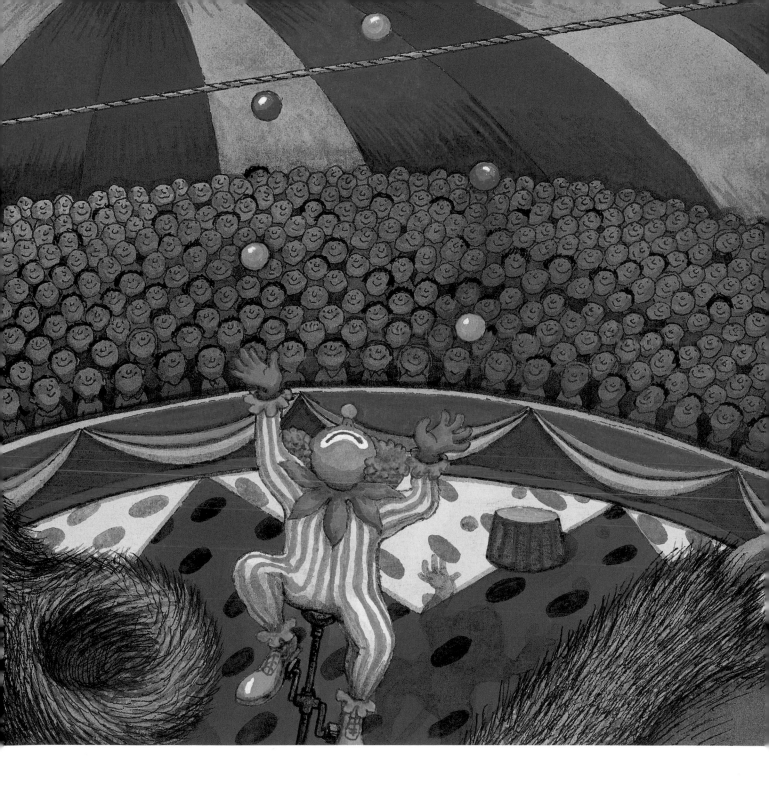

People clap and cheer

and shout for joy

as the stone twirls through the air.

But the stone remembers

the thump of wild apples

falling to the earth.

Its heart breaks a little.

It wants to go home.

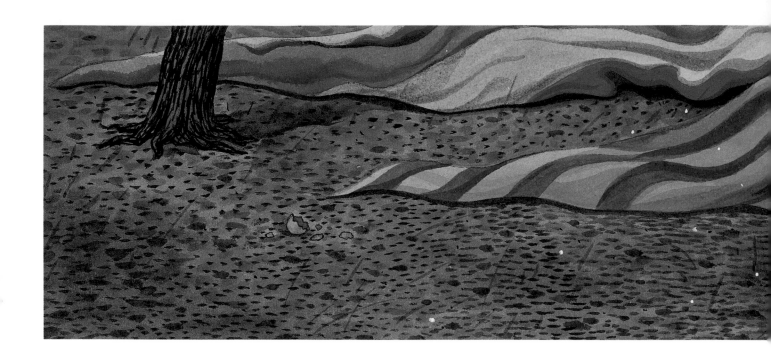

Carelessly, the clown

tosses the broken stone away.

Thick snow covers it with cold.

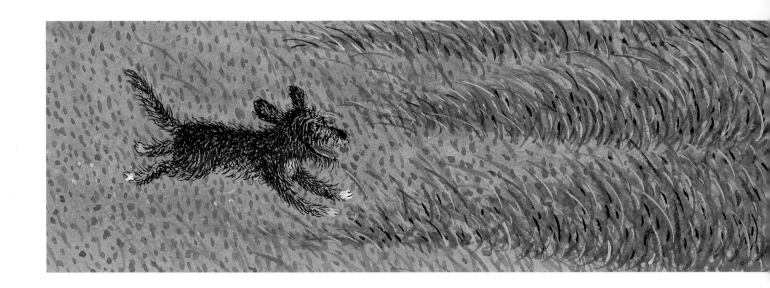

In spring, grass grows up

to hide the stone.

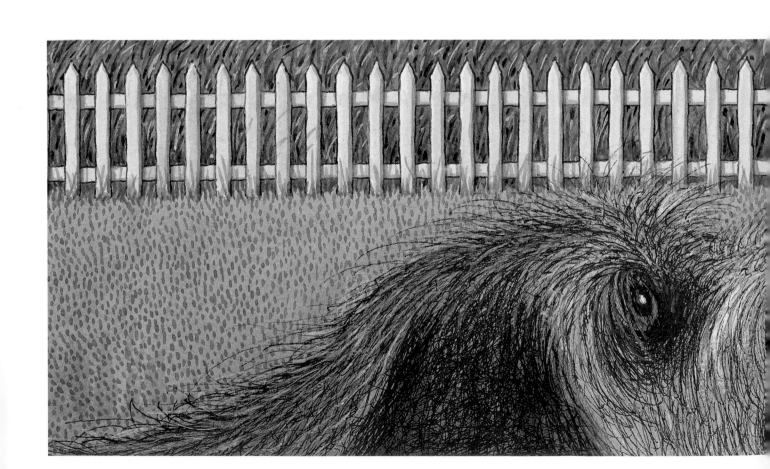

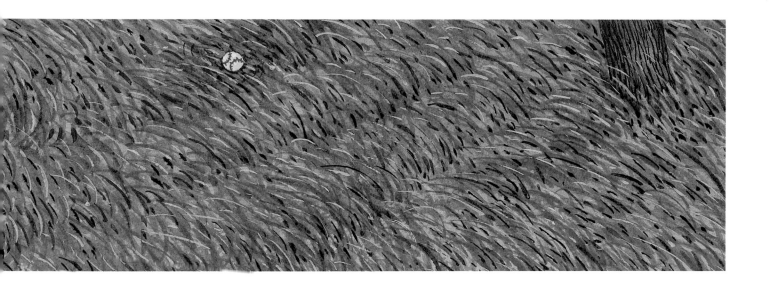

One day a boy throws a ball.

But his dog brings something else back to him.

The boy carves and polishes the stone

to make a gift.

The lonely blue stone lies

over a heart warm with love.

The stone's heart breaks a little.

And since first love rarely lasts,

the girl's heart breaks as well.

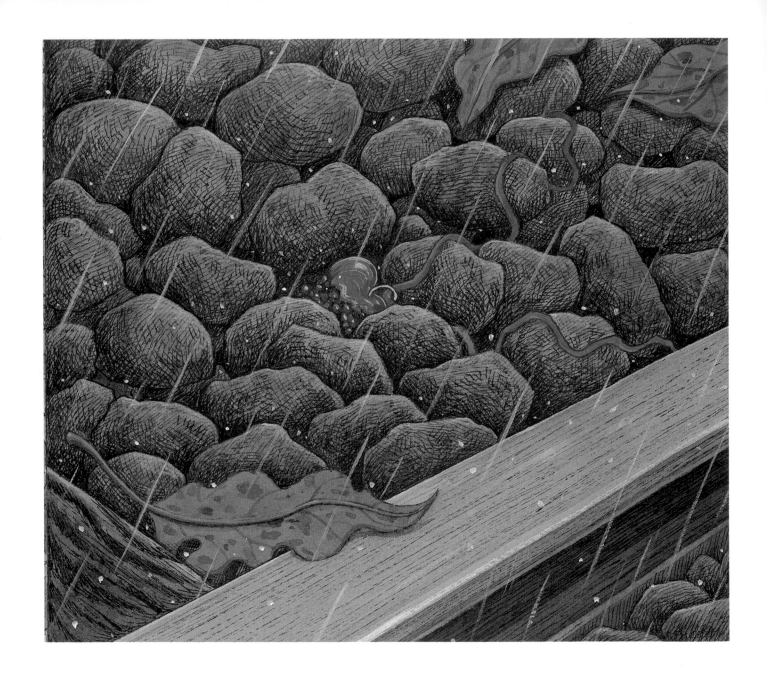

With each passing train

the blue stone cracks again

until only a few grains of sand are left…

...light enough to rise

with a breath of summer wind.

What's left of the stone

floats over a town.

It drifts across an ocean.

At last it returns to the forest

and sinks down to lie

with its other half

where it has always belonged.

A year goes by,

ten years go by,

a hundred years go by,

a thousand years go by,

ten thousand years go by…

And a blue stone lies peacefully

in the heart of a forest.

TO MY FATHER AND MOTHER.

———————

JIMMY LIAO was born in Taipei, Taiwan and received a degree in design from the Chinese Culture University. He worked as an illustrator in the advertising industry for twelve years, but left to pursue his own creative endeavors. He is the author and illustrator of over twenty-five hugely popular books that have been translated into English, French, German, Greek, Japanese, Korean, and Thai. His first book for Little, Brown, *The Sound of Colors*, has been adapted into a stage play, as well as a motion picture directed by award-winning Hong Kong director Wong Kar Wai.

Jimmy has said that painting is how he expresses the way he views the world; looking at his work is like seeing into his heart. A cancer survivor, he hopes that his work can brighten the lives of others. He lives in Taipei, Taiwan, with his wife and daughter.

This edition is an adaptation based upon the English translation of the work titled *The Blue Stone,* by Jimmy Liao, originally published in Chinese by Locus Publishing Company in April 2006. Original work copyright © 2006 by Jimmy Liao.

Little, Brown and Company

Hachette Book Group USA • 237 Park Avenue, New York, NY 10017 • Visit our Web site at www.lb-kids.com

First U.S. Edition: April 2008

Library of Congress Cataloging-in-Publication Data
  The blue stone: a journey through life / by Jimmy Liao ; English text adapted by Sarah L. Thomson.—1st ed.
      p. cm.
  Summary: A beautiful stone that has lain in the forest for thousands of years is split in two, and one half goes on a long journey through many places, many owners, and many transformations, its heart continually breaking as it longs for home.
  ISBN 978-0-316-11383-0
  [1. Rocks—Fiction. 2. Homesickness—Fiction.] I. Thomson, Sarah L. II. Title.
  PZ7.J575255Blu 2008
  [Fic]—dc22   2007031073

10 9 8 7 6 5 4 3 2 1

SC / Manufactured in China

The illustrations for this book were done in watercolor.
The text was set in Mahsuri Sans, and the display type is Sackers Gothic.